These monkeys are for Kerri. I couldn't do it without you.
— A. L.
For Emery, Eden, and Lauren.
— M. F.

SIMON & SCHUSTER BOOKS FOR YOUNG READERS
An imprint of Simon & Schuster Children's Publishing Division
1230 Avenue of the Americas, New York, New York 10020
Text copyright © 2015 by Adam Lehrhaupt
Illustrations copyright © 2015 by Matthew Forsythe
SIMON & SCHUSTER BOOKS FOR YOUNG READERS is a trademark of Simon & Schuster, Inc.
For information about special discounts for bulk purchases, please contact Simon & Schuster Special
Sales at 1-866-506-1949 or business@simonandschuster.com.
The Simon & Schuster Speakers Bureau can bring authors to your live event. For more information
or to book an event, contact the Simon & Schuster Speakers Bureau at 1-866-248-3049 or visit our
website at www.simonspeakers.com.
Book design by Lucy Ruth Cummins
The text for this book is set in Matchwood WF.
The illustrations for this book are rendered digitally.
Manufactured in China
0715 SCP
2 4 6 8 10 9 7 5 3 1
Library of Congress Cataloging-in-Publication Data
Lehrhaupt, Adam.
Please, open this book! / Adam Lehrhaupt ; illustrated by Matthew Forsythe.
pages cm
"A Paula Wiseman Book."
Summary: The animals appearing in a book, excited to be "saved," beg the reader
not to close them in again.
ISBN 978-1-4424-5071-4 (hardcover) — ISBN 978-1-4424-5072-1 (eBook)
[1. Books and reading—Fiction. 2. Animals—Fiction. 3. Humorous stories.]
I. Forsythe, Matthew, 1976– illustrator. II. Title.
PZ7.L532745 Ple 2014
[E]—dc23
2013038336

first edition

PLEASE, OPEN THIS BOOK!

BY
· ADAM
LEHRHAUPT

PICTURES BY
MATTHEW
FORSYTHE

A PAULA WISEMAN BOOK
SIMON & SCHUSTER BOOKS FOR YOUNG READERS
New York London Toronto Sydney New Delhi

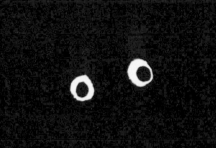

Hello?

Finally!

Quick.

Someone, turn on the light.

You opened the book.

We're saved!
We're saved!

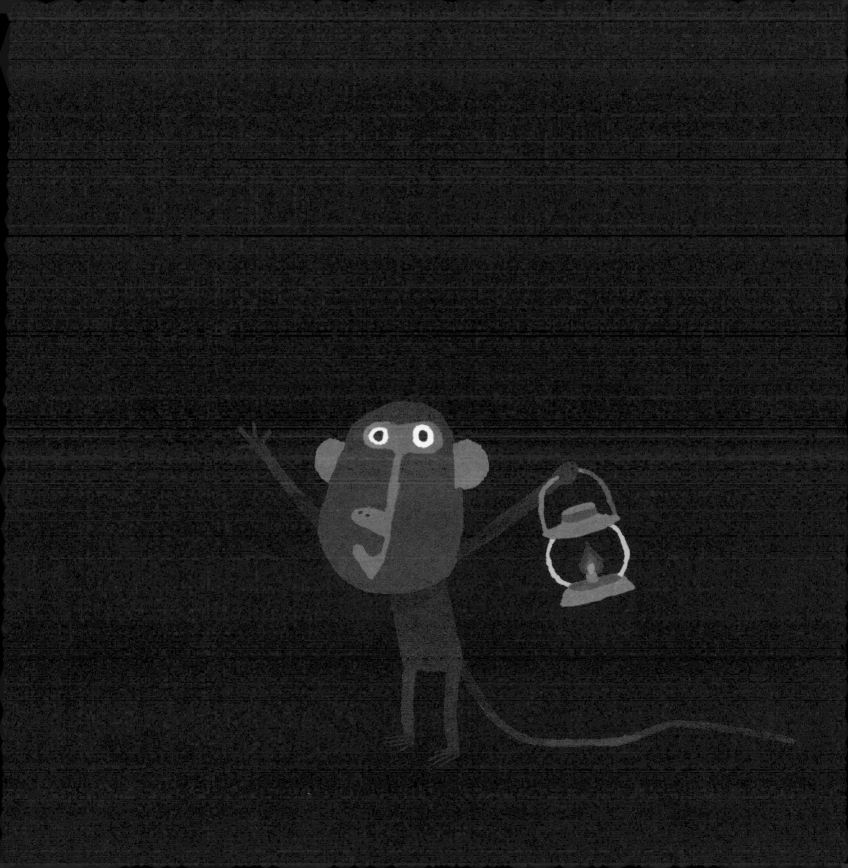

Do you know what happened?
Someone **closed** this book!
They just slammed it shut!
With us inside!

Why would anyone close a book?
Especially a **really good**
book like this one.
You should leave it open.

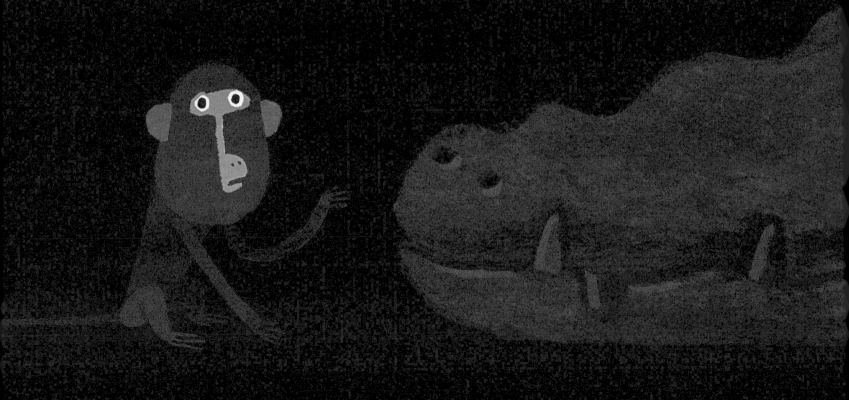

This is what happens when you close a book.

And he's been in there for days.

The worst part?

They completely destroyed this

perfectly good banana!

We worked hard for that banana.

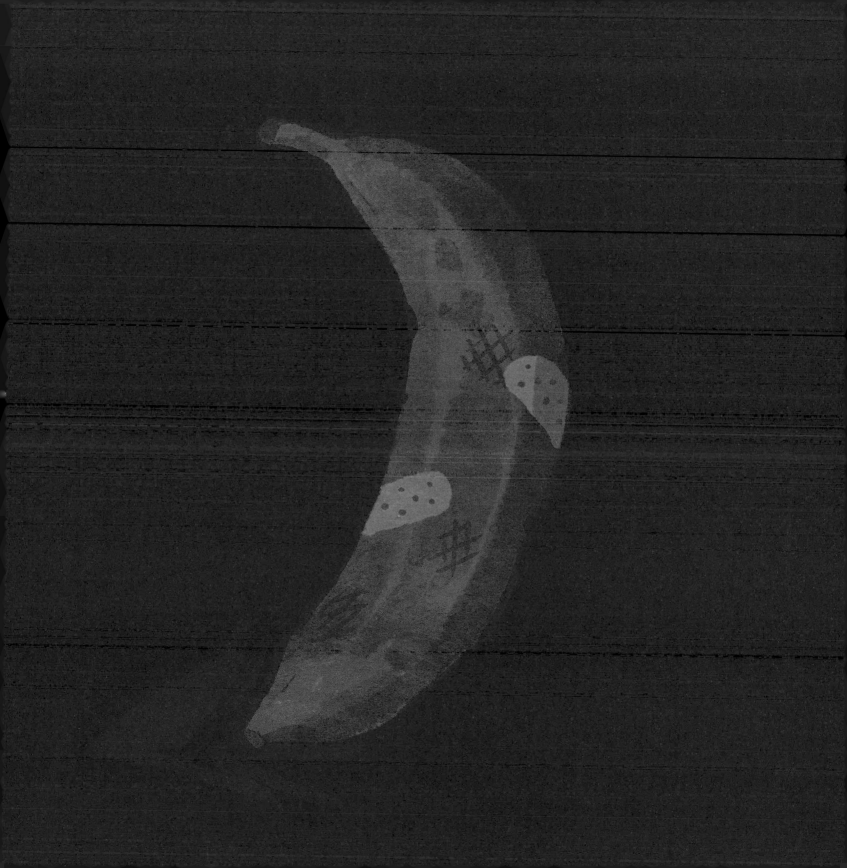

We saw who did it. He looks just like this.
Have you seen him?

We're still fixing things from last time. So you should leave this book open. Just put it down.

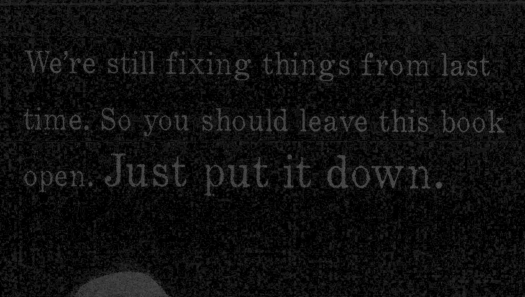

Step away
from the book.

We can change the story.
We'll write something
with a hero and heroine.
You'll like it.
It will be a good story!

You'll want to leave it open.

You turned another page!
Don't you know what will happen?
If you keep turning pages,
you'll close the book.

We'll be trapped . . .

again!

You wouldn't do that to us,
would you?

We'll be good,

Promise.

We'll give you the
rest of this banana.
There's still
a little left.
The other half
was tasty.

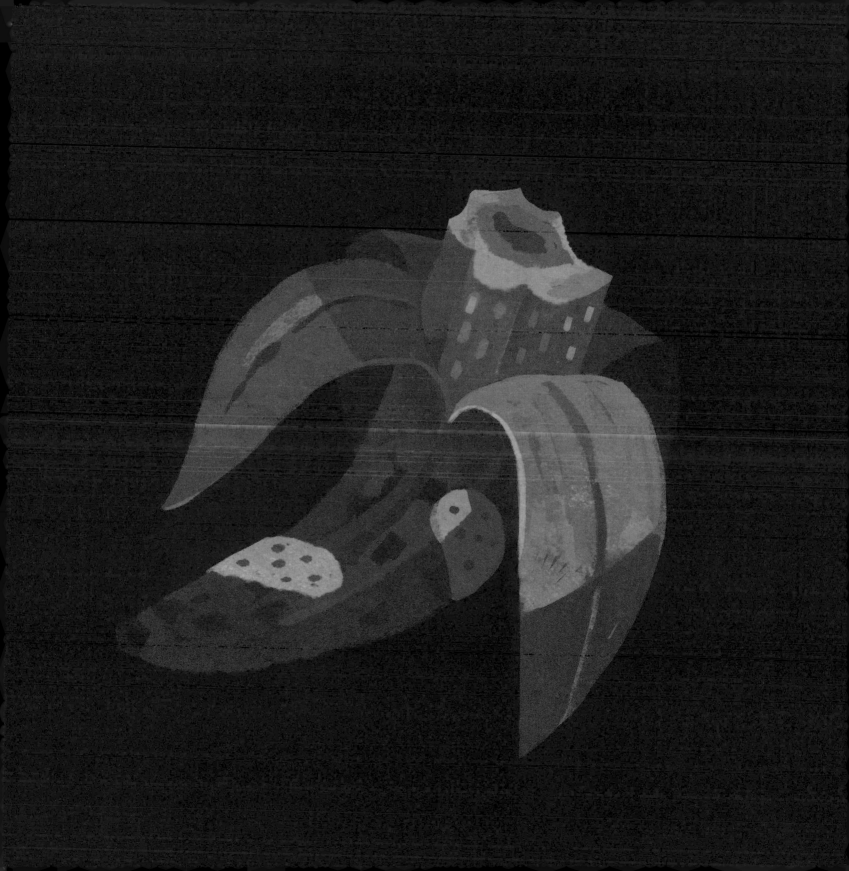

You could get stuck too.

Did you think about that?

Don't be this person.

Don't be a book closer.

Stop!

Don't turn this page.

You're almost at the end.

If you go any further, we can't go with you.

THIS

BOOK

WILL

BE . . . .